This book is your passport into time.

Can you survive in the Age of Pirates? Turn the page to find out.

TIME MACHINE 4

Sail with Pirates

by Jim Gasperini
illustrated by John Pierard
and Alex Nino

A Byron Preiss Book

BANTAM BOOKS
TORONTO · NEW YORK · LONDON · SYDNEY · AUCKLAND

For Mary Jane

RL 3, IL age 10 and up

SAIL WITH PIRATES
A Bantam Book/August 1984

Special thanks to Ann Hodgman,
Anne Greenberg, Len Neufeld, Lucy Salvino,
Shirley Feldman, Pauline Bigornia, and Ann
Wheeler.

Book design by Alex Jay
Cover painting by Dave Stevens
Cover design by Alex Jay
Mechanicals by Studio J
Typesetting by Graphic/Data Services

"Time Machine" is a trademark of
Byron Preiss Visual Publications, Inc.
Associate Editor: Ann Weil

ISBN 0-553-23808-6

Published simultaneously in the United States and Canada

Bantam Books are published by Bantam Books, Inc. Its trademark,
consisting of the words "Bantam Books" and the portrayal of a
rooster, is Registered in U.S. Patent and Trademark Office and in
other countries. Marca Registrada, Bantam Books, Inc., 666 Fifth
Avenue, New York, New York 10103.

PRINTED IN THE UNITED STATES OF AMERICA

0 9 8 7 6 5 4 3 2 1

ATTENTION TIME TRAVELER!

This book is your time machine. Do not read it through from beginning to end. In a moment you will receive a mission, a special task that will take you to another time period. As you face the dangers of history, the Time Machine often will give you options of where to go or what to do.

This book also contains a Data Bank to tell you about the age you are going to visit. You can use this Data Bank to help you make your choices. Or you can take your chances without reading it. It is up to you to decide.

In the back of this book is a Data File. It contains hints to help you if you are not sure what choice to make. The following symbol appears next to any choices for which there is a hint in the Data File.

To complete your mission as quickly as possible, you may wish to use the Data Bank and the Data File together.

There is one correct end to this Time Machine mission. You must reach it or risk being stranded in time!

YOUR MISSION

Your mission is to find the wreck of the richest silver ship ever to sink in the Caribbean sea, and to bring back some of the treasure.

In July 1641, the richest Spanish galleon ever to sail the Caribbean left Vera Cruz, Mexico. Her name was *Our Lady of the Pure and Immaculate Conception*. The Spanish sailors called her *Concepcion* for short. She was a big, powerful ship, but she sailed slowly. . . for good reason. She carried one hundred and forty tons of silver in her hold. The king of Spain, heavily in debt, waited eagerly for this immense treasure to arrive.

In August 1641, the *Concepcion* reached Havana, Cuba. One month later, along with a fleet of other ships, she departed for Seville, Spain.

She never made it.

Off the coast of Florida, a tropical storm almost sank the *Concepcion*. Searching for shelter, the crew sailed her south. She hit a reef, or sunken island, and broke apart. Her passengers escaped on rafts before the ship sank. Months later, they tried to find the reef again.

They never found it.

The king of Spain was furious, but there was nothing he could do. The fortune in silver was lost in the ocean.

For forty years it sat somewhere on the floor of the Caribbean Sea, until William Phips, a sea captain from the British colony of Massachusetts Bay, went looking for it. He found the wreck of the *Concepcion* and carried a good deal of its silver treasure to London.

But he didn't get it all.

Ever since Phips's voyage, treasure hunters have wondered if another fortune might be waiting in the sea. No one knew exactly where Phips found his reef. They only knew it was somewhere to the north of the island of Hispaniola. Today that island is divided into two countries: Haiti and the Dominican Republic.

You decide to head for the Bahamas in 1684. William Phips stopped there on his way to search for the treasure, and he's the only one you're *sure* can lead you to the silver.

Your mission: Find the lost *Concepcion* and bring back some of its treasure!

 To activate the Time Machine, turn the page.

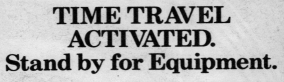

TIME TRAVEL ACTIVATED.
Stand by for Equipment.

THE FOUR
RULES OF
TIME TRAVEL

As you begin your mission, you must observe the following rules. Time Travelers who do not follow these rules risk being stranded in time.

1. You must not kill any person or animal.

2. You must not try to change history. Do not leave anything from the future in the past.

3. You must not take anybody when you jump in time. Avoid disappearing in a way that scares people or makes them suspicious.

4. You must follow instructions given to you by the Time Machine. You must choose from the options given to you by the Time Machine.

EQUIPMENT

You take with you an old-fashioned knapsack with a few useful items, including a knife, sailor's clothes, and a map of the Caribbean in the 1600s.

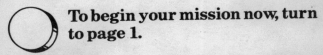

To begin your mission now, turn to page 1.

To learn more about the time to which you will be traveling, turn to the next page.

DATA BANK

Florida

20 September 1641
Havana

Concepcion
departs
23 July 1641
Vera Cruz

Mexico

Providence

The more a time traveler knows about a time period, the easier it is to explore that period safely. Here are a few important facts about the Caribbean area in the seventeenth century:

1) Silver isn't the only valuable thing you

Hurricane
28-30 September 1641

N

Bahamas

New
Providence

Turks and
Caicos

Handkercher Reef

Anegada

Isabela

Samana Bay

Cuba

Vaca

Hispaniola

Jamaica

Puerto
Rico

Virgin
Islands

Port Royal

might find. Be on the lookout for ambergris, a rare substance made by whales, which is used in making perfume. It may look like a strange gray rock floating in the water.

2) The first settlement in the New World was called Isabela. It was founded by Christopher Columbus on the north coast of Hispaniola.

3) Scurvy is a disease that used to kill many sailors. It is caused by a lack of vitamin C. Long after the 1600s, sailors learned how to wipe out scurvy by eating lemons or limes on long voyages.

4) The word *buccaneer* is now another word for pirate, but there once was a difference. The first buccaneers hunted wild pigs on Hispaniola.

5) After the buccaneers began raiding ships, they used several islands as bases, including Port Royal, Jamaica. Port Royal sank into the sea after an earthquake in 1692.

6) A privateer is a kind of pirate licensed by one king to raid the ships and towns of anoth-

er. Of course, to the king whose ships are being raided the privateer is just a plain pirate!

7) The front of a ship is the bow; the back is the stern. A small sail at the bow—called the foresail—is very important in steering the ship. The main storerooms are called the hold; the sailors' sleeping quarters are in the forecastle.

8) Someone left alone on a desert island as punishment is said to be marooned. A Maroon can also be an escaped slave living off in the hills.

9) When sailors rebel and take control of their ship from the captain, that's a mutiny.

10) The first English colony called Providence in the Caribbean was established on a small island near Nicaragua. It was destroyed by the Spanish in 1641. Soon afterward, the town of New Providence was built in the Bahamas. New Providence was also temporarily destroyed by the Spanish, just before William Phips visited it in 1684.

DATA BANK COMPLETED. TURN THE PAGE TO BEGIN YOUR MISSION.

 Don't forget, when you see this symbol, you can check the Data File in the back of the book for a hint.

ou're standing in the hot Caribbean sun in New Providence, the Bahama Islands. It's April 26, 1684.

"Hey, Lucky!" A man gets up from the sand under a palm tree and waves in your direction. He must mean you, because you're the only one around.

He walks up painfully, leaning on a rough crutch made from a tree branch. "You got out of here just in time, Lucky Century, afore the Spanish come to burn us down."

Who is Lucky Century? you wonder.

"What did you come back here for, anyway?" He looks at you with a puzzled grin. "Don't you remember me—Hiram Robertson?"

"Well, uh . . ." You explain that you want to sail with a Captain Phips.

"Phips! Why, he's looking for sailors. Hurry on down to the harbor. He's about to sail!"

You walk with Robertson, who asks strange questions about a ship called the *Timely* and about pirates. He seems surprised that you don't understand.

The town is a mess. People are replacing damaged roofs and doors in the few houses still left standing.

"There's Phips now," says Robertson. "Oh, Captain!" A tall, powerful-looking man stares you up and down.

"A little young to put to sea," he finally says.

"I may be young," you say, "but I'm eager! I want to learn everything there is to know about sailing."

"All right, sailor, but listen here: we're after sunken treasure. Plenty for everyone if we find it, but no pay at all if we don't. Hard biscuits and salt beef, rough weather and too much sun."

"That's fine with me," you tell him.

"Where's Jim Teal?" the captain calls. He tips the man with a crutch for finding you. A boy about thirteen puts down a barrel and runs up. The captain waves his hand at the web of ropes hanging from the nearest ship's masts. "Teal," he says, "show our new hand the ropes."

"Glad to, Cap'n Phips!" Teal grins at you. "This way," he says, taking your arm at the elbow.

He pinches it hard as soon as the captain has his back turned.

"Now listen here, Century," he hisses in your ear. "I'll show you the ropes, all right. If you cross me I'll see you hang from one of 'em! You do what I say—no back talk. When I say jump, you jump! You understand?"

You look this guy straight in the eye and nod. Why is he so nasty? And why does every-

body here think they know you? Well, you decide, if they're all going to call you Lucky Century, you might as well use that name.

As Teal explains the ship's routine, the ship turns and points out to sea. The strongest sailors pull the anchor cable up by winding it around a wheel called a capstan.

"Weigh *ho*, away! Haul away, my *Rosie*," the sailors sing. With each O sound they give the capstan a push. "Weigh *ho* away, haul away *Joe*."

The captain rings a brass bell on top of the forecastle when the anchor lifts off the bottom. Sailors waiting far up the masts let the sails fall when they hear the bell. The square sails fill out with wind.

You glide out to sea, part of the crew of the *Rose of Algeree*.

Turn to page 8.

ou're still in Vera Cruz, Mexico, but now it's July 1641. You see the same shacks and sandy streets as when you left the Vera Cruz of almost forty-two years from now. The big white church is brand-new now, and the bell tower is firmly in place.

Long lines of mules carrying heavy leather bags wind down the hills from Mexico City. In the plaza sits a mountain of silver in bars, plates, and bags. Men load it onto ships bit by bit. You go up to an official watching over the loading.

"Is this all the silver going to Spain?"

"Is this all? You joke! This is just the tail of the donkey." Something about his voice is familiar—yes! It's Francisco Granillo. A younger man now, and of course he doesn't recognize you—he's never met you before!

"The king's silver," he continues, "is split between the lead ship, the *San Pedro y San Pablo*, and the rear ship, *Nuestra Senora de la Concepcion*. Then there are thirty more merchant ships with silver. How much silver? On the *Concepcion* alone there are four million pesos! One hundred and forty tons!"

He looks at you carefully. "With so many ships, we need many sailors. You know the sea? We could use you aboard the *Concepcion*."

Perfect! That's the ship whose eventual grave you're here to find. You agree immediately and ride out to the galleon on a boat so loaded with silver it barely clears the waves.

You sail on the *Concepcion* across the Gulf of Mexico toward Havana, Cuba. The voyage takes almost a month. It's hard to imagine that this whole ship, so full of life, will soon sink under the waves. But not yet—up ahead is Cuba, and soon you'll be exploring the biggest Spanish port in the Indies: Havana.

To Havana—*vamos!* Turn to page 14.

You decide it would be fun to be a pirate. You go to sleep in your hammock without saying anything to Phips.

You dream that a snake is wrapping its coils around you, squeezing tighter and tighter.

"Aha!" someone shouts, waking you up. It's Captain Phips. He's found out about the mutiny! You try to jump to your feet, but you can't. There's a rope tied tight around your hammock! Most of the sailors are tied up the same way.

"Now what have we here?" Phips says, striding around the room. "A group of mutinous moths, all wrapped up in their own cocoons! Fishes like to eat moths. Maybe I'll feed you to them!" He stalks out, followed by a few loyal sailors.

This wasn't so smart. You know Phips found the treasure, so the mutiny couldn't have succeeded. How could joining these greedy mutineers have helped you, anyway?

Your hammock swings in a dark corner. No one would notice if you jumped back in time. Better try again.

 Jump back in time. Turn to page 1.

After three days at sea, Captain Phips calls you to the bow. "Somewhere up ahead," he says, "is the Handkercher Reef. On a map, it looks like a handkerchief, but it's really jagged rocks and coral."

He shields his eyes. "I think the Spanish galleon broke to pieces somewhere on that reef. The same thing could happen to the *Rose of Algeree*. It's your job to see that it doesn't!" He hands you a long rope with a piece of lead on its end.

You drop it into the sea and let the rope out until it hits bottom. When it hits, you pull the rope back up. You count the lengths of rope from the end of one outstretched hand to the other: this distance is called a fathom.

"Ten fathoms!" you call. Still plenty of water between the ship and the bottom. You keep a sharp eye on the water ahead. "Nine fathoms and a half!"

A far-off cry comes from the lookout in the crow's nest: "Boilers ho! Reef ho!"

In the far distance, you can just make out the white-tipped line of a reef.

Phips anchors off the reef. You search for three weeks, but there's no sign of the wreck.

You're swinging a little in your hammock one night, trying to get to sleep. The forecastle is crowded with noisy sailors.

"A fool's errand this Phips is on," says one of the sailors.

"Aye, and the more fools we for going with him!" says another. "Old Spanish silver sunk who knows where, and treasure ships aplenty sail these waters all the time. No treasure, no pay—that's what old buccaneer Henry Morgan used to offer, but he knew where to find *his* silver. He took it right from the Spanish!"

Teal jumps up on a table. "Why don't we take the ship and sail it where we please?"

"Aye, the boy's right. Let's be pirates! Leave the fool Phips on an island. Maroon him! Who's with us?" You close your eyes and pretend to be asleep.

"Tomorrow at daybreak we take the ship," someone cries. "And them that don't join us can join—the fishes!"

These sailors are planning a mutiny! Should you tell Captain Phips about it or keep quiet and join their pirate band?

 Join the mutiny. Turn to page 7.

 Tell Captain Phips. Turn to page 12.

Phips kicks the mutineers off the ship in Port Royal, Jamaica. They stalk away, muttering curses. You decide to explore the town before the ship sails again.

As you pass a noisy sailors' bar, a man in a police uniform grabs your arm. "There you are!" he shouts. "Come with me."

The policeman drags you to a jail. "Found another one," he tells a friend. "A runaway indentured servant, name of Century. Ran off with some black slaves as belongs to Master Throneberry." Jim Teal stands watching by the door.

"You're mistaking me for somebody else," you say. "I'm a sailor, just come in on the *Rose of Algeree*. Tell them, Jim!"

Teal just laughs. They throw you in a damp cell with a dirt floor and no windows.

Well, you think, sitting in the darkness, it's time to jump in time. Captain Phips is having trouble finding the treasure. Why not help him out—find out exactly where the ship went down, and meet him again somewhere? You could jump to where the Spanish ships loaded up with silver—in Vera Cruz, Mexico.

Jump back almost a year to the port of Vera Cruz. Turn to page 20.

When everyone is snoring, you sneak out and tap quietly on the captain's door.

"By thunder!" Phips growls when he hears the news. "I'll show these pigs who's master here."

Phips finds some loyal sailors, and you sneak into the forecastle. Very quietly you coil a rope around Teal, sleeping in his hammock. The other men do the same to the rest of the mutineers. Phips gives a signal, and you pull the ropes tight!

Teal and the others yell and struggle, but they're tied securely in their hammocks.

"Now, what have we here?" Phips says, striding around the room. "A group of mutinous moths, all wrapped up in their own cocoons. I'm told, my friend Century, that fishes like to eat moths."

You follow him out on deck.

"Confound it!" says Phips. "Now we'll have to sail to Port Royal to get rid of them and find a new crew. Well, maybe in Jamaica we'll find some better clues about where to find the treasure."

Turn to page 11.

14

You're standing near the docks of Havana, Cuba, where the crew of the *Concepcion* is enjoying a month of *fiesta*. It's September 20, 1641. You notice an oil lamp burning near the waterline of the *Concepcion*. You creep through the shadows and jump out into the light.

"What are you doing?" you ask sternly.

An old black man reaches under the waterline and pulls something out of the wood. "I am collecting shipworms," he says.

He holds up a long white slug with a shell on one end. "You sail to Spain on this ship?" He puts a finger in his curly white hair and twirls it. "You are *loco*—crazy. Look!" He points to the hull. Little holes run through the planks.

"Too long this ship sits in these waters, and no repair." He points to the sky. "The hurricanes come soon. The last safe time to leave for Spain is twentieth August, and here it is twentieth September!"

Bad news! Maybe you should stay in town and enjoy the fiesta some more.

 Sail with the *Concepcion*. Turn to page 28.

 Stay in Havana. Turn to page 23.

You're right on the edge of a cliff! You step back. The cliffs line a natural harbor on Providence Island. Several tall-masted ships sway gently in the harbor breeze. You walk down a narrow path into the first town called Providence. It's May 24, 1641.

A cheering crowd of sailors surrounds the entrance to a bar. You push through to see what's going on. Two men face each other across a small table.

"So it's double or nothing, eh?"

"Right. But I don't trust the way you roll them dice, Calico Joe!"

"Well, and do I blame you? Let's get somebody else to do it." He looks at you. "Hey, mate! Are you lucky?"

"That's my name," you say. "Lucky Century."

"Well, then! Roll me dice, matey!" He holds out a couple of big, bumpy-looking dice with crowns and anchors instead of dots. You roll them across the table.

"Crown me . . . crown me, little darlings!

Ha!" says Calico Joe. The other man turns white and slowly moves away. Calico Joe rakes in his money with a laugh. "Pull up a stool, my lucky matey, and have yourself a drink!"

You learn that the sailors all come from a ship called the *Sea Hawk* moored a few yards away. "About time we paid a wee visit to the Spanish, don't you think, boys?" says Calico Joe. The others pound the table in agreement.

"Are you pirates?" you ask.

"Pirates?" Calico Joe exclaims, laughing. "No, mate, we're privateers! The English king gave us a paper what says we can raid the Spanish all we like. Hands off your English towns, but who cares? The Spanish have all the silver!"

Suddenly the table flips over. The privateers go tumbling to the ground.

"Get thee behind me, Satan!" A stern man in black with a tall hat and carrying a Bible points a bony finger at the sprawling men. "Thou lovest not the things that be of God, but those that be of men!"

"Ow," says Joe, stumbling to his feet. "This new Puritan minister is worse than the last one!"

"Look at you," says the Puritan. "Grown men playing Satan's games! While your ship lies there idle and the shipworm eats its hull. And spreading your corruption to a mere

child!" He grabs you by the ear and drags you off.

"The Devil smiles on an idle child," he says, hitting you over the head. He takes you down to a ship called the *Morning Star*. "Put this youngster to work!" he says to the captain, a stocky man named Broadstreet, and stalks off.

Broadstreet stares after him, amused.

"He's not that bad a chap, really, but he's got a lot to learn." The captain puffs on his pipe. "He acts as if he's in the other Puritan colony, up in Plymouth, Massachusetts Bay. There the cold, cold winter puts the fear of God in you, sure." He looks you over. "But if you'd like to help us load up, you're welcome."

You help load crates of lemons, limes, and other supplies on the *Morning Star*. This is a trading ship, you learn, about ready to sail to Cuba by way of Sant' Jago. It's a long trip, and Broadstreet is careful to take plenty of supplies in case something goes wrong.

A sailor comes running up, his arm dripping with blood.

"Better finish up your loadin', Captain. The Spanish are invading!"

"Blast those privateers!" says Broadstreet. "I knew that someday the Spanish would get fed up with their raids. Now we'll all pay!" The work speeds up, and the ship is soon set to go. Just in time, too. You hear the sound of galloping horses as Spaniards waving swords ride through the town. Townspeople try to trip the horses with spears.

"You!" Captain Broadstreet calls. "Want to come with us?"

Calico Joe runs up. "Well, mate, your luck's still good. We've got the *Sea Hawk*'s sails all trim, and we're off to green Tortuga. Will ye sail with us? Quick, we've got to get out of here!"

 Fly with the *Sea Hawk*. Turn to page 33.

 Follow the *Morning Star*. Turn to page 24.

You're in Vera Cruz, Mexico. It's May 26, 1683. The town is so quiet you can hear the mosquitoes buzz. The hot sun bakes the dusty wooden shacks, the empty sandy streets running down to the sea, and a big white church. Where is everybody?

You walk down to the edge of the sea.

"Buenos dias!" says an old man, motioning you to sit down with him. "I am Francisco Granillo. Sit down! No one should be out in the sun at siesta time. Why are you here?"

"I'm looking for the ships," you say. "When will they load the treasure galleons?"

"Ho! You are too early. The ships come once a year. The rest of the time, Vera Cruz is a city of the shadows."

"Don Francisco!" A girl runs up shouting. "A sail! The fleet has come!" Suddenly the town comes alive. Men and women run down to the sea to watch. A dozen ships approach the harbor from the north.

Just as suddenly, the rejoicing stops. The smiles disappear. Old Francisco mutters under his breath.

"What's wrong?" you ask.

"Those ships," he says slowly. "They are not ours! They are French ships, and Hollanders."

"What's wrong with the French?"

He looks at you as if you're crazy. "The

French? They are pirates, of course!" He shakes his head. "They will destroy our town. In 1641, we destroyed the English raiders, in Providence. Now the raiders have returned! Once Spain was strong," he says sadly, "but all empires must grow weak one day. Run for your life!"

Longboats full of men waving pistols approach the shore. The people of Vera Cruz grab what they can carry from their houses and run for the hills. A cannonball hits the tower of the old white church, and the big bell comes crashing down.

You run as fast as you can. A storeroom door opens and a man runs out, carrying a very heavy bag. You jump through the open door, slam it shut, and crouch in the darkness. You can hear screams and shouts outside as the pirates destroy the town.

The door bangs open and a thin, bearded man runs in. He has a torch in one hand and a sword in the other.

"Aha!" he cries, throwing his torch to the floor and grabbing you. He twists your arm behind your back and puts his sword to your neck.

"Where is the silver?" he hisses in your ear. "Tell me, quick!"

"I—I don't know. I'm just a visitor here!"

"Ha! You lie. Shall I give you a smile, a nice red smile, from ear to ear?" He presses the sword harder against your throat.

A second pirate bursts in and surveys the

room with his torch. "Here it is!" he shouts. The other end of the room is piled high with bars of silver gleaming in the torchlight. "Mark this down," the new pirate shouts. "I claim all the silver in this room as my share of the plunder."

"Not so fast, Grammont." The first pirate pushes you away and waves his sword. "I was here first. This is mine."

"And if, my dear Van Horn, this is the only silver storehouse?" They both have their swords up now.

"Then, gentle sir, I'm afraid you will be very sad. *En garde!*" The pirates battle through the room.

Maybe it's time to be on the trail of your own silver. You could jump back in time to the year the *Concepcion* left for Spain—1641. Do you want to jump back to this same town, Vera Cruz, or to the island of Providence old Francisco spoke about?

The straw-covered floor smolders from the torches. The pirates don't seem to care as they lunge and parry with their swords.

Jump back in time forty-two years.

 Stay in Vera Cruz. Turn to page 4.

 Go to Providence. Turn to page 15.

You're at a fiesta in the streets of Havana when you notice two men in Spanish soldiers' uniforms looking at you oddly. You start to sneak away, but they run after you.

"You! You look like a sailor. Want a job?"

"No, thanks," you say. "I like your city very much. I plan to stay."

They grab you by the shoulders and carry you down the street!

"The king's armada sails today, to escort the silver fleet. Sorry to spoil your fun, but the king needs sailors." They hang a uniform around your shoulders and hand you a sword. A line of recruits is marching onto a ship. They put you on the end of it.

"Hup, two! Hup, two!"

"Have a nice trip," they call, "soldier!"

 Turn to page 32.

You sit sipping lemon-
ade, watching an island grow bigger as the
Morning Star sails closer. It's about time! For
a week you've had nothing to do. The ship just
sat there, with no wind to push the sails along.
Now the wind is back, and you're heading for a
Spanish settlement. You help pile cloth, nails,
gunpowder, and other European products onto
the deck.

A small boat comes to meet you. Broadstreet
tosses you a gun. "When they come aboard,"
he says, "point this at the one who does the
talking."

"In the name of King Phillip," says one of
the Spaniards as he steps on the deck, "I command you to depart! No Lutheran unbelievers
are allowed to sail in Spanish waters."

"You see these sailors with guns?" says
Broadstreet, pointing at you. "I am taking you
hostage!"

You're surprised. You didn't think Broadstreet was a pirate!

"I will kill you all and fire my cannons on
your town unless you let me trade with you."

"Oh, no!" says the Spaniard. He doesn't look very worried. "Don't kill us. We have ginger, pearls, and sugar which we will give you to ransom our lives. Here is a trading license, which you have forced us to give you against our will."

"Isn't this ridiculous?" says Broadstreet. "The poor Spanish colonists! The officials in Spain won't let them trade with us legally, but they have no other way to get the things they need. So we have to pretend to *force* them to do business." He's not a pirate after all—he just has to pretend to be one!

One of the Spaniards pours a dark brown liquid from a pitcher. Broadstreet takes a sip and passes the glass to you. "Here," he says. "Taste this. The Spanish say it's very valuable, but I don't know. I've never seen it before."

You take a sip. Chocolate! You pretend to be drinking it for the first time.

"What do you think?" Broadstreet asks. "Should I buy it? Do you think anybody will want this stuff?"

"Don't worry," you say. "I'm sure this will be very popular someday."

Soon you're sailing north again, toward Cuba.

"Century!" a sailor calls. "It's your turn to be lookout. Climb the mast to the crow's nest!" You grab hold of the rope ladder and climb

hand over hand. You pass the bottom sail, then the middle one. You stop to catch your breath, and look down.

It's a *long* way down! Well, you think, if it's shorter to go up than to go down . . .

One of the ropes breaks under your feet! You hang on with your arms, kicking in the air to find the ladder again.

Made it! You crawl out on the wooden platform and hug the skinny pole. A flag flutters just above your head. You force yourself to look over the edge of the crow's nest.

You're right above the ocean! The ship slides over a wave, and you swing back over to the other side. And you're supposed to spend six hours up here!

What are you doing up here, anyway? you wonder. This isn't helping you find the treasure! Maybe you should jump in time. Then you wouldn't have to crawl back down that pole.

You could jump ahead in time and meet up with the *Concepcion* before it leaves Havana for Spain.

Jump ahead a few months to Havana. Turn to page 14.

Half a hundred great ships sail in formation across the sea. You're riding the *Concepcion* on her last voyage—what better way, you think, to find out where the reef she hit might be?

The best way to get to Europe, the sailors know, is to let the Gulf Stream carry them up the coast of Florida and across the wide Atlantic. Unfortunately, it flows through a dangerous area. Many ships have been smashed to bits on the reefs of Florida and Bermuda.

One week out from Havana, the sky turns black. A storm is coming. The crew ties everything down securely.

You go below to your hammock and try to sleep, but the ship rolls too much. People are getting seasick, and you don't feel so well yourself.

Someone pounds on the door, shouting, "All hands on deck!"

You hurry upstairs. A wall of churning water is rolling right at the ship! The waves are higher than the deck. Up the ship goes, lifted by the wave, until you're riding on a white-topped mountain of water. Then, with a stomach-churning lurch, the *Concepcion* slides down again into a deep watery valley.

"Tie yourself down!" A sailor tosses you a rope, and you tie it around your waist. You do it just in time, for the next wave passes right over the deck!

You get a mouthful of salty water. You're swimming in the ocean! *Which way is up?* You can't even tell where the ship is anymore. You pull on the rope around your waist and catch hold of a sail. When the waters finally pass, you find yourself hanging ten feet up the main mast. You watch as barrels, sails, and a chicken coop full of squawking birds float away.

The wooden mast shakes under your fingers.

As you look up, the gigantic mast, the size of a tall tree, splits in two. The top part dangles crazily in a jumble of ropes and splinters. Someone just under you hands you an axe.

"Chop the ropes! Chop them all away!" You tie yourself to the stump of the mast and chop at the tangle of ropes until the mast is free.

The small foresail at the bow of the ship rips to shreds and blows away. Now the ship spins with its side to the waves and tilts completely over! Water pours in over the sides before another wave straightens the ship up again.

"We must lighten the ship!" says Francisco Granillo. Sailors bring cargo up from below and throw it into the sea. But not, you notice, any silver.

Another ship of the fleet goes by the other way.

"Help!" people on your ship shout. "Mother of God, help us!"

"They cannot save us," cries a priest. "No one can but the Lord. The waters will take our bodies. Entrust your souls to God!" People drop to their knees and pray to the statue of Our Lady of the Conception, bolted to the deck.

Another mountain of water hits the ship. When it clears, the statue of the saint is gone.

"Oh, no! It is a sign of doom!"

You don't want to stay on this ship if everyone on it's going to die! Maybe you should find somewhere safe to jump in time. The Bahamas are not far away.

Jump ahead forty-three years to the Bahamas. Turn to page 50.

Ride the *Concepcion* to her doom. Turn to page 36.

You're now a soldier of the king of Spain! The army ship has twice as many cannons as the normal galleon, but no silver to weigh it down. You follow the *Concepcion* in the fleet, slipping back to protect stragglers from dangerous raiders who live in the nearby English colonies of Georgia and Carolina.

One week out from Havana, a hurricane hits. The ship pitches for two days and two nights. Cannons break loose and go smashing across the deck. No one knows your location, but you soon find out.

SKREEEACK! You've hit a reef off the Florida coast! The wind and waves smash the ship against the rocks. You find yourself floating in the sea, holding a wooden chest to keep afloat.

Enough of this! You're cold and wet, and nothing but hostile Indians awaits you in the Florida of 1641. The safest place you can think of nearby is nice, warm New Providence.

 Jump ahead forty-three years to New Providence. Turn to page 50.

You slump down on a coil of rope in the shadow of the *Sea Hawk*'s limp and useless sails. There's been no wind at all for almost a week. The ship is becalmed, lying motionless on a wide sea flat as glass.

"Oh, me aching legs!" says Calico Joe. He sits down next to you. His skin is oddly yellow, you notice, even though he's sunburned.

"I don't know what's wrong with me," you say. "I just don't feel like doing anything."

"None of us has much wind in our sails, mate," says Joe with a weak grin. "Let me have a look at your teeth." He pulls down your lip and runs his finger along your gums. It hurts!

"A pretty fair set o' teeth you have," he says. "I hope you get to keep 'em."

"Keep them?"

"Hope so. Do they feel loose? If they do, you've got the scurvy, mate! All of us on board are gettin' it. And if the wind don't pick up soon, losing our teeth will just be the beginning. The scurvy can do a lot worse."

"What causes scurvy?" you ask.

"It's the shipboard plague. Nobody knows

what causes it. I got an idea it's something in the food, but I've been eating salt beef and sea biscuit all my life. You only get scurvy on long trips."

You don't want to lose your teeth! Maybe you should jump in time directly to the treasure ship's port.

You haven't had a piece of fruit or a fresh vegetable since you came on board; the ship left in an awful hurry. You remember the lemons you were loading on the other ship. You get a candle and go below the deck to see if anyone thought to store some on the *Sea Hawk*.

You open a barrel to look for lemons, and you feel something soft. It squeals. Rats! Huge gray rats are gnawing through the barrels, eating the food inside them. You jump back and drop your candle.

Now you can't see anything, but the room is filled with squealing sounds. The rats crawl on you, jumping on your shoulders. You throw them off, but they're everywhere! You could jump ahead in time to get away—back to the port the silver ships left from. You've got to get off this scurvy-plagued, becalmed, and rat-infested ship!

 Jump ahead twenty-two years to Vera Cruz. Turn to page 20.

The storm spins and batters the *Concepcion*. The mate, your friend Francisco Granillo, stands up and shouts against the wind.

"Though our main mast is broken, there is still hope. If we can rig a new foresail, we can control the ship! Who will help me try?"

"It's no use," cries one man. "And too dangerous!"

"Dangerous?" says another. "Who cares? We are already dead men."

You volunteer along with a few other sailors. To reach the foresail you must crawl across the slippery, sloping deck, so six of you tie yourselves together by the waist with a long rope. Several times you lose your footing and almost fall into the sea, but at last you manage to tie a piece of canvas to the dangling ropes. It's a desperate last chance—but the ship comes about to point into the wind.

From the depths of despair the sailors raise a cheer.

"Are we not sailors? Are we not proud Spaniards? Man the pumps!"

For a day and a night you struggle to keep the ship afloat. On the second morning the sun breaks through the clouds.

The *Concepcion* is still afloat, but a ship with no main mast cannot go very fast. There are no Spanish ports nearby to seek help from. No one quite knows where the ship is, but Don Juan de Villavicencio, the admiral, decides to sail south to Puerto Rico. Unfortunately, that's at least a thousand miles away!

The ship limps along as best it can. One day you hear shouts coming from the admiral's cabin. Francisco Granillo comes storming out, gives a kick at a spare sail, and sits down with you.

"Idiots!" he exclaims. "Those pilots! You know how they got their jobs?" He rubs his fingers together. "A little silver can buy many jobs. But it cannot buy the wisdom to do them well! They think we are due north from Puerto Plata. Turn south, they say. *Caramba!*"

"Where do you think we are?"

"At least three hundred miles to the west. *Nombre de Dios!* If we turn south now, we will hit the dangerous Handkercher Reef!"

A few nights later, you're asleep in your hammock when a sudden jolt throws you to the floor.

SKREEEINK! You stumble about in the darkness, trying to find your clothes. Another terrible noise, and you're thrown against the wall. The ship is tilting. Which way out of

here? You run across the wall—into a pool of water! You grab your things and scramble up to the door.

A man rushes past you with a sword stuck through his chest. He collapses. There's only one lifeboat left on board, and the passengers are fighting over who will be in it.

Admiral de Villavicencio comes out of his cabin. "Stop!" he cries. "We're on a reef. Firmly stuck, so we won't sink tonight. Wait until morning, and we'll build rafts for everyone!"

You spend a cold, unpleasant night huddled on the deck above the waves. At dawn, the tide goes out, and the sailors groan at the sight of their ship. The stern is caught on two big rocks. The bow is already sunk beneath the sea. The remaining masts shoot out at a crazy angle. All around you are what look like the stumps of old trees: a dismal forest of coral.

Well, here you are. You not only found the wreck, you were riding on it when it hit the reef. When everyone has left, you can dive for treasure at your leisure. You sneak off across the rocks where no one can see you.

Jump six months ahead to search for treasure. Turn to page 47.

You're back on board the wreck of the *Concepcion*, November 4, 1641. Strange—it's been half a day for you, only an instant for everyone else!

You help the carpenters rip up the deck. You sew sails together and tie up a few empty barrels to float rafts. Every so often the ship gives a shiver and slips a little farther into the water.

The pilot points to a strange-looking instrument called a sextant at the sun.

"We are at nineteen and three quarters degrees forty-five minutes latitude," he says. "The only reefs at that latitude are northeast of Anegada, in the Virgin Islands. We should sail our rafts east or southeast to land in Anegada."

A second sailor fiddles with the sextant. "Yes, you are correct about the latitude," he says. "But the best way to sail is southwest. A little farther, but we will reach Puerto Rico, where there are Spaniards to help us."

"Give me that sextant," says another man. He makes his own calculations. "We are be-

tween twenty degrees thirty minutes and
twenty-one degrees. We must be in the Handkercher Reef! The best way to sail is west, to
Cuba."

"Why don't you figure out the longitude?"
you suggest. "Then you would really know
where we are."

They stare at you. "Be my guest," says the
pilot, with a grunt. "Do you know how? I don't.
Nobody does. The day sailors can figure that
out, we'll be a lot safer!"

Don Juan de Villavicencio believes the pilot
and decides to sail southeast. He takes the
only boat, which he fills up with important
passengers, including Francisco Granillo—
but not you. Rafts are going in three different
directions. You check your map carefully to
decide which one to get on.

 Sail east. Turn to page 44.

 Sail southwest. Turn to page 52.

 Sail west. Turn to page 54.

t's April 24, 1494. You're on the north shore of a large island, exactly where you were in 1641, but the ruined house has disappeared. The bay is filled with ships. Men in pointed helmets chop down trees, clear brush, and build shelters. You creep through the forest to get a closer look, careful not to let anyone see you.

"Stop work!" someone shouts. "The admiral will speak to us before he sails."

A man stands before a crowd by the edge of the bay.

"Friends!" he says. "Spaniards! Colonists! I sail today to the west, in search of the mainland of India."

"God speed you, Admiral," shout the colonists. India? you think. He's got a long way to go!

"The colony you build is very important. It is the first Spanish settlement in this part of the world. The great city you are building I will name after our glorious ruler, Queen Isabela."

"Long live the Queen! Hurray for the city of

Isabela! Long live our Admiral, Christopher Colombus!"

Columbus! A boat takes him off to one of the ships. So the ghost town is Isabela! According to your data bank, Isabela was on the island of Hispaniola. But does that tell you enough to lead Phips to where the treasure is?

You feel something cold and sharp pressed against your back.

"What are you doing here?" says a soldier. He pokes you with his spear. "You're not a colonist. And you have too many clothes for an Indian. Tell me who you are, or die!"

No sense trying to explain! You take off for the thickest part of the forest. Time to jump, and quickly.

Jump to Jamaica in 1684 to tell Phips what you've learned. Turn to page 96.

You've been sailing east on a tiny raft for four days now. There's still no land in sight.

Could you have missed the island of Anegada? Are you heading for Africa, thousands of miles away? The food runs out, but the raft sails on. The passengers begin to argue.

"We should have gone south," says a man in a wet velvet coat.

"But the pilot said east," a sailor replies. After two days of hunger, everyone agrees to turn south. After another day, you sight land.

"An island," you shout. "Palm trees! Coconuts! Food!" The sailors stumble ashore and collapse. You manage to break open a coconut and greedily gobble it down.

Then you hear a shout. Out of the woods come a hundred nearly naked Indians. They poke you in the ribs with long spears, shouting in a strange language. The tips might be poisoned, so you do what they want!

They herd you all to the center of the beach. An Indian diver from the *Concepcion* stands near you.

"You're an Indian," you say. "Ask them what they want."

"I am an Arawak," he says, "the last of my tribe. Once all these islands were Arawak. No more. These"—he points to the dancing guards with disgust—"these Caribs are monsters. They killed the Arawak and took our land."

"Do you understand what they are saying?" you ask.

"Yes." The Arawak looks at you sadly. "They cry, 'Meat! Meat! Look at all the meat we found!' The Caribs are cannibals."

The Caribs are poking you again, pushing you down the beach toward their village. You've been invited to dinner, it seems!

You decide to refuse the Caribs' invitation. To continue searching for the treasure, you'd better jump in time!

You pass a field of high grass on the way to the village. You make a sudden leap into the grass, just far enough to be out of sight of the Caribs chasing you.

Jump to the future of the cannibal island. Turn to page 66.

ou're standing on a rock just above the surface of the water. Six months have gone by since the *Concepcion* sank here. Only a few seagulls keep you company. Far below the water's surface, you can see the front half of the *Concepcion*. There's plenty of treasure stored in either half. Silver, here you come!

You strip off your clothes and jump into the warm water. You take a deep breath and kick off toward the bottom. It's farther away than it looked. You've almost reached the wreck when you start running out of air! You kick madly for the surface and burst into the sunshine.

You rest and try again. And again. Finally, you manage to reach the deck of the ship. Green things grow all over it. You reach inside a hole and pull something out.

It's a weedy, eaten-out skull! You drop it, kick your way to the surface, and jump out onto your rock.

The treasure is locked away inside the ship. How are you going to get to it? You have no

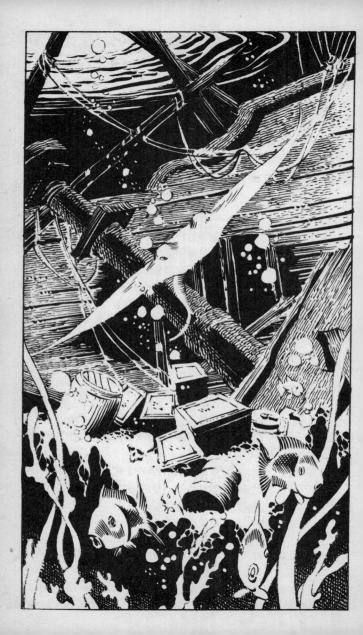

trained divers, no equipment, nobody to help you if you get hurt. It looks as if you'll need Captain Phips after all. Perhaps you should jump in time—now that you know where the reef is, you can find Phips and show him the way.

But how would you ever lead Phips back here? You don't even know what reef you're on. Your search is not over yet. You should have stayed and taken a ride on one of the rafts. Then if you'd landed on an island, you'd have known which way to come back.

You get an idea. Suppose you jump back six months to the very second after you jumped here? Nobody would notice you'd ever been gone!

Jump back to join the survivors of the *Concepcion*. Turn to page 40.

Glug! The water's warm, at least, but what are you doing in the ocean? You grab hold of a floating glob of gray stuff, but it's not much of a life preserver. Luckily you're not far from shore, so you swim in to a beautiful beach, carrying the floating mass you found.

You sprawl out on the white sand and rest. It feels good to relax a bit, far from shipwrecks, pirates, and crazy people. Down the coast you can see the town of New Providence, in the Bahamas. It's January 10, 1684.

Someone's coming down the beach. Oh, no! It's that nasty kid from Captain Phips's boat, Teal. You get ready to punch him if he tries anything.

"Hi!" he says without seeming to recognize you. "New around here? I'm James Teal." He holds out his hand. You shake it, wondering at his friendliness. Then you realize—you must be back *before* your first adventure, so of course he doesn't know you!

"Just what this island needs," he says sarcastically, "another beachcomber. That's what

I am. But don't ask me to give you any clues on how it's done. That—" He stops, staring at the gray lump you're holding between your knees.

"Say," he says offhandedly, "that's a funny rock you have there. Maybe a dead mollusk. What do you want for it?"

"I don't know."

"I'll give you a real Spanish piece of eight I found." He shows you a crude, lumpy sort of coin with a cross on it.

You rub your hand on your gray-brown lump. It feels slightly greasy. Why does he want it so much?

You shake your head.

"How about two? Say, suppose I tell you where I found 'em? There's probably an old wreck nearby, and you can go diving and find a whole potful of treasure."

Now that sparks your interest. Maybe the wreck is the *Concepcion*! Should you trade him your lump for his information?

 Sell Teal your gray-brown lump. Turn to page 63.

 Tell him no deal. Turn to page 57.

You're waiting on the tilting stern of the *Concepcion* as the last raft is loaded. The boards tilt more beneath your feet. The ship is sinking! The raft glides away. You jump into the water and swim after it.

"No more! The raft is overloaded!" Someone pushes you away, but you hang on. Another man pulls you aboard.

"Come back!" shouts a man still standing on the ship. But the raft sails on to the southwest. The ship gives one last creak, splits in two, and slips beneath the waves. How will you ever find it again? Well, you think, if you hit land sailing southwest, you should be able to sail northeast from the same spot to find the reef.

For two days the raft pushes clumsily along. There's nothing to see but sea and more sea. At the end of the second day, you run out of food and water.

"Look! Land! We're saved!" someone cries at last. You sail west along the northern coast of a large island, looking for a place to find water and hunt food. But which island is it?

"This must be Puerto Rico," says the pilot of the *Concepcion*.

"Hah!" says a soldier, "What do you know? You're the one who got us into this mess." He points a pistol at the pilot's ear. "I say this is Hispaniola. And if I'm right, there's no excuse for your wrecking our ship on a reef in calm weather. The king will want to see you hanged, and I'm going to make sure you are!"

You pass the mouth of a wide bay.

"Look! A town!" You sail up the bay toward the settlement and stumble off the raft.

Where are the people?

Ruined houses overgrown with weeds. It's a ghost town. No one has lived here for many years.

BANG! A gun fires right behind your head. You jump to the ground. Another shot goes off. A man leaps over some rocks and runs off into the jungle. You hear shouts.

"The pilot! Stop him. The pilot is running away!"

But the pilot gets away.

Behind the ruins of an old well, an ancient path leads up into the mountains. The Spanish decide to follow it in hopes of finding a settlement.

You stay behind. If you jump into the past, to when people were living in this ghost town, you could find out exactly where this island is. Then you'd have an idea of where the ship went down—since the raft came southwest, the reef must be northeast of wherever this is!

Jump back in time to when people lived in the ghost town. Turn to page 42.

You're sitting on a raft so weighted down with people that the water is up to your chest. You've been sailing slowly west for three days. You're terribly sleepy, but whenever you doze off you get a mouthful of seawater. Worst of all, there are no mouthfuls of *drinking* water left.

"I can't stand it!" croaks a woman. She puts her mouth to the waves and takes a drink from the sea.

"No!" her husband cries. "That's salt water. It will kill you!" She knows, but she no longer cares. She screams and jumps into the sea.

"My poor Carla! No sleep, no water—she has gone mad." Her husband dives in and swims after her. They float away.

When will you get to Cuba? you wonder. You take out your map to check. It's over a thousand miles away! This raft will never make it that far.

Another man screams as he's pulled from the raft. He disappears beneath the waves. In his place, the water is stained with red. A grey triangle zips through the water ahead of you.

Sharks! They're swimming right onto the

raft, picking people off one by one. You feel something slip along your leg . . . got to get out of here, fast! Luckily you have another way to get to Cuba.

 Jump ahead in time to safety in Vera Cruz. Turn to page 20.

You don't trust this Teal at all, so you take your rock into town to find out what it is. New Providence is a bustling, rough, but tidy little town—not at all like the smoking wreck you remember from your first visit.

You see a sign: "SHIP'S CHANDLER. Hiram Robertson, Owner." Teal darts ahead of you and blocks the door.

"This is my final offer," Teal says. "I'll give you all the money I have in the world, and I'll be your servant for six months. C'mon, mate! It's just a rock, anyway."

"Sorry," you say.

"Half of it's mine," he says angrily. "You would have just thrown it away if I hadn't noticed it!"

"You could have offered me a deal like that before, but it's too late now," you say. "Out of my way!"

"I'll get you for this!" he shouts, and stalks off. Well, now you know why he was so nasty to you the first time you met him.

You enter the shop, and put your lump on

the counter in front of Mr. Robertson. His mouth drops open as he picks it up.

"D'ye know what this is? Why it's *ambergris*! Eleven, twelve pounds—you're rich!"

"I am?"

"Sure. This stuff is more costly than gold!"

You ask Mr. Robertson to sell it for you, and he agrees with pleasure. Poor Robertson—you can't tell him that the Spanish will soon burn down his shop.

"By the way, mate, where do ye come from?"

"The twentieth . . ." What are you saying? ". . . century," you finish awkwardly.

"The Twentieth Century? What's that, a ship? Oh," he says, winking. "I get it! No pryin' questions. Don't ye worry. A lot of people around here don't talk much about where they be comin' from or where they be goin.' For one reason or another, eh? We'll call you Century. Lucky Century!"

Robertson takes you out on the docks and waves his hand at the ships.

"Now, if I was you, I'd spend my money on a good ship. Things are changin' in the Caribbee. The Spanish don't control things anymore. French, English, Hollanders are all buildin' colonies. There's more and more business for a trading ship. What do you think?"

You *could* buy a ship—and sail wherever you please! Sail it to Hispaniola and look for the treasure of the *Concepcion* on your own. "Are there any ships for sale?" you ask Mr. Robertson.

"It just so happens," he says, "that there is one. Right over there—the frigate *Timely*. With the money from the ambergris, you could buy her, outfit her with goods and crew, and still have change for breakfast!"

In the next few days, that's exactly what you do. With Mr. Robertson's help you buy the same sort of equipment you remember Phips had. You hire a captain and crew to sail with you. Soon you're out at sea!

It's a lot more fun standing on the bridge with the pilots than sweeping out the hold. You're proud of the *Timely*. All yours!

"Vessel sighted off the starboard stern!" your captain calls one morning. He hands you a telescope. "They've signaled that they have a message for us."

"A message?" You hold the long metal tube to your eye and adjust the focus. The ship comes into view. A signal flag flutters from one of its masts.

"Could be a trick. They could be pirates! Should we turn and wait for them or try to get away?"

You're suspicious. What kind of message could they have for you? Nobody even knows you in 1684! You tell the captain to signal that you don't have time to wait for messages.

As you watch through the telescope, the other ship's signal flag comes down. In its place rises a black flag with something white on it. The wind changes, and you see what's on the flag: a *skeleton*! One bony hand holds a dripping sword, and the other a bottle of rum. It's the Jolly Roger.

"They're showing their true colors now," the captain says. "I know that ship! It's Captain Joseph Bannister in the *Golden Fleece*. He's the most bloodthirsty pirate in the Caribbean." Your captain shouts to the sailors. "Up main sail, men! We need all the speed we can get!"

All the sails the *Timely*'s masts can hold are raised aloft, but the pirate ship is still faster. You hear a loud boom. A cannonball smashes the railing in front of you.

The cannonballs whiz through the air. A shot tears the *Timely*'s main sail in two. Now the pirate ship is only yards away! The cannons stop.

"*YAAAIIEAAGH!*" The pirates scream a bloody war cry as they jump from their ship onto yours. Swordfights rage from bow to stern.

This is terrible. What are they fighting for? Your mission isn't so important that these sailors should die for you. You can find another way to the treasure.

"Stop!" you shout over the awful noise of battle. "Stop fighting!" Your sailors pause. You see a look of surprise on some of the pirates' faces.

"I own this ship," you say as loudly as you can, "and I surrender! Please stop fighting."

Your sailors grumble, but they don't seem that unhappy to put down their swords.

A thin man with a black eye patch on one eye stalks up to meet you on the upper deck. He looks you slowly up and down.

"I am Joseph Bannister," he says proudly, "captain of the *Golden Fleece*. And now, it seems, master of this ship, too." He lifts up your chin with the point of his sword.

"When I say I have a message, you should listen! But you have saved me the trouble of killing you. I give you a choice. Will you join my pirate band, or shall I keelhaul you and leave you on the first island I pass? You have one minute to decide!"

 Sail with the pirates. Turn to page 77.

 Choose to be keelhauled. Turn to page 90.

You hand the strange lump to Teal. He takes you down the beach a couple of miles. There's a ship anchored a long way offshore.

"This is where I found the Spanish coins," Teal says. "Good luck in finding the wreck they came from!" He hoists the lump onto his shoulder and runs off.

For the next few days you camp there at the beach, looking for signs of the wreck of the *Concepcion*. You find a few old nails, bits of broken pots, lots of seashells, and a strange sort of comb. But no coins. One day a small boat leaves the anchored ship and comes ashore.

"Hello!" you say to the first man who gets out. "What are you doing out there?"

"Divin', of course." He unloads some empty pots. Other men go off looking for water. "That's where the Spanish galleon *Las Maravillas* sank about ten years ago. Ye can still find a few bars o' silver if ye look hard enough."

Las Maravillas? That's not the ship you're

looking for. Well, of course: the *Concepcion* went down north of Hispaniola, and here you are in the Bahamas, hundreds of miles away!

"Does everybody in New Providence know about that wreck?" you ask.

"Yer a fool if ye don't. Folks have been divin' on her since the year she went down."

You march off toward town. You can hardly wait until you get your hands on that cheat Teal!

The town of New Providence is busy and neat, nothing like the shot-out mess you remember from your first visit. You guess that the Spanish should be coming to raid it soon. You stop a woman carrying a basket of fish.

"Excuse me, ma'am. Do you know a boy named James Teal?"

"Lucky Jim Teal!" she exclaims. "He's been playing high and mighty ever since he struck it rich."

"He's rich?"

"Sure. He's the boy who found that lump of ambergris. Bought himself a big house, he did. Here he comes now!"

A horse and carriage pull up to the fanciest house on the street. Teal sits there smirking at you, dressed in silk and velvet.

"What have we here?" he says loftily. "A beachcomber!"

"You cheated me, Teal," you say.

"*Mister* Teal to you," he replies. "Them that don't know when they've got something good don't deserve to keep it."

You look at his house and imagine what it will look like when the Spanish burn it down.

"Enjoy it while you can," you say with a smile. "It may not last long."

"What's that supposed to mean?"

"What will you give me for some interesting information?"

He laughs. "I don't need to trade with fools like you anymore," he says with scorn. He tethers the horse to a post and walks proudly into his house.

A fleet of ships turns into the harbor from the north.

BOOM! They're firing cannons at the town. People are running everywhere.

"The Spanish!" they scream. "Run for your lives!" Cannonballs come whistling through the air. You duck as one smashes Teal's door down.

Well, no sense staying here. Time to jump back to 1641, the year the *Concepcion* sailed. New Providence didn't exist then, but Providence did.

 Jump back 43 years. Turn to page 15.

ou're alone on a small island. It's February 17, 1684. The beaches are deserted, but you see a ship on the horizon. You jump up and down and wave your arms. Will it see you?

The ship anchors offshore, and a boat is let down. When it gets to shore, a man steps out.

"I am Captain De Graaf," he says. "I see that you are wanting transportation. Well, that is our business, in a manner of speaking, no? We could take you to Port Royal. But what payment will you be giving us, eh?"

"I'm a sailor," you say. "Do you need an extra hand?"

"I am sorry, we are having plenty of sailors. But! You could sign indentures—be my servant for a couple years maybe, and so pay your debt for the ride." It doesn't seem like a very good deal, but you agree.

The boat is full of empty water kegs. You help Captain De Graaf load casks of water on the ship. They sure need a lot of water!

"The cargo is thirsty," says De Graaf. "Four thousand miles we are sailing from the Gold Coast. They drink like horses. Go below and give them water."

You hear a low moaning sound from below the deck. What kind of cargo is this ship transporting?

Halfway down the stairs, you stop.

You're on a slave ship! Men and women are chained up on racks so narrow they have no room to stand up. You go to them in turn, handing each a cup of water. Their heavy chains rattle as they take the cup. One man is so weak he can't even hold the cup. You hold his head and help him drink.

"This other one's dead," says a sailor. "And this one over here." They unchain the dead bodies, take them up on deck and throw them overboard. How can the sailors do this? They act as if they're carrying cows or sugar in the hold.

You have the worst trip you ever hope to have on the way to Jamaica. You try to help the poor Africans as much as you can, but you can't set them free. You hear their cries and groans everywhere you go. Every time you bring them food and water, you have to look away from the rows of frightened and angry eyes.

At Port Royal, the slaves are marched ashore. People passing by don't pay much attention—it's just another cargo come from Africa. Men come to inspect the "merchandise." They check the slaves' teeth and feel for broken bones.

One slave spits in a planter's face as he tries

to check his teeth. Crack! goes the whip of a guard against his bare back.

Guards prod a few slaves up on top of a wooden platform.

"Here's a fine selection!" cries the auctioneer. "Who will make me an offer for these prime specimens? Africa's best, gentlemen! Strong and agile."

"Fifteen pounds a head," offers one man. "Fifteen pounds Jamaican!" scoffs the auctioneer. "Gentlemen, are you going to let him get away with that? A steal at fifteen pounds! Fearsome warriors in their native jungle— with a little seasoning they'll cut through sugarcane like a hurricane!"

The poor slaves stand there in the hot sun. Some look angry, some scared and bewildered. How can people treat others this way?

"You! Century!" the slave-ship captain calls. He has your indenture papers in his hand. "Here's the fellow," he says to a thin man in a white hat carrying a cane. "A good worker, good with the slaves."

"Century," he says to you, "this is Master Throneberry. He's your new master now, for the next five years. Good luck."

So he's selling you, too—until your indenture years are finished!

Go to the Throneberry Plantation. Turn to page 72.

You're lost in the jungle of Hispaniola. It's November 7, 1641. Well, at least you're on the island closest to where the treasure ship went down!

You hear a low grunting sound ahead of you. Out of the weeds steps a huge wild pig. It must weigh five hundred pounds.

It stares at you with its beady little eyes and bares its long fangs. It's coming after you!

You run, leaping through tangled weeds with the grunting pig at your heels.

POW! The pig behind you falls with a crash. Someone has shot it! You look around.

Lowering his smoking gun is the strangest man you've ever seen. His jacket, his pants, and even his long beard are black with what looks like dried blood. A dozen long knives hang from his belt. What are they for? You wonder who he is, but if he's here to kill you you're not sure you want to find out! Should you hide yourself and jump? He pulls out a knife and steps over the pig.

 Escape to New Providence. Turn to page 50.

 Find out who this is. Turn to page 87.

You get up early. Today's the day everyone on the Throneberry plantation starts to cut the sugarcane. You walk down to the fields.

A young slave named John is already there. He hands you a long, flat knife called a machete.

Other slaves and servants arrive, each carrying a machete. Sugarcane looks like giant grass. You hack at the thick stalks. They're hard to cut, even with the sharp machetes.

By the end of the day you're "bone tired," as John calls it. He invites you to have dinner in the slaves' quarters. It's crowded but very clean and busy. John introduces you to his mother, father, and three sisters.

After dinner John takes you to a corner. He leans over and whispers. "Century. My friend, right? Could you do me a big favor?"

"Sure," you say. He reaches under a pile of wood and brings out something hidden.

"I seen you readin' that book you have with you." He looks at you eagerly. "Could you teach me how to read? Please!" He shows you his precious secret. It's an old-fashioned spelling book. "Master, he don't want slaves to know nothin' except how to cut cane. But there's so much of the world I wants to know about! Here." He opens the book. "That's an *A*, right? What's the rest of it say?"

"*A* is for the apple," you read, "that Adam ate." There's a picture of Adam and Eve by a fruit tree in the Garden of Eden.

Suddenly the room is quiet. The door swings open, and Master Throneberry walks in, followed by a boss slave called the slavedriver. John quickly shuts his book and sits on it.

"Well, John," says Throneberry, "so we're having a little chat with our friend Century! What's that you're sitting on, John?"

"Nothin'."

"Nothing? Why don't you stand up and let us see?" He prods at John's leg with his cane.

"Get up!" the driver commands. "You stand up when the Master asks you!" John stands up slowly. Throneberry snatches the book.

"Well, well. A spelling primer! Now what could that be doing in the slaves' quarters?"

"That book's mine!" you say.

"Yours! Well, you're my servant, so what's yours is mine." He walks over to the fireside, ripping pages from the book.

"John, no!" cries John's mother, as John runs across the room and plucks the book from the fire. Throneberry grabs him by the shoulder. John hits him across the face!

Throneberry steps back in amazement. The
driver grabs John and drags him to a pile of
logs.

"You little devil!" shouts Throneberry. "You
know the penalty for striking a white man!"
The driver holds John's arm against a log and
picks up a machete.

"Which hand was it, Master?" the driver
shouts.

"The left."

"Don't you worry none, Master. That hand
ain't never going to strike you again!" He
raises the machete over John's hand. John
twists and kicks.

You can't just let them cut his hand off! You
run up and grab the machete from the driver's
hand. "Get out of here," you yell, waving the
machete at Throneberry and his driver. "Let
him go and get out of here!"

"Well, Lucky Century," says Throneberry,
as he backs away. "We'll see how lucky you are
when I get through with you!" You slam the
door in his face.

"You've got to run for the hills," John's father says. "They'll be watchin' the door, but
we'll cover for you." John's mother and sisters
move silently about, gathering food and
clothes and tying them in a sack. John kisses
his mother goodbye and turns to you.

"There be *Maroon* towns out in the woods,"
he says with a grin. "Maroons are runaway
slaves livin' free. Come on!" John's father

opens the door, and you all rush out into the night. People whoop and dance and run in every direction. They all carry sacks just like yours, so that in the confusion no one will know which way the real runaways are going.

"Hurry!" John says as you plunge through the forest.

"Will we really be safe with the Maroons?" you ask when you catch your breath.

"I hope so. Them Maroons have a leader named Nanny. She's a sorceress! She can see the future. She can catch them bullets in her teeth and throw 'em right back!"

Off in the distance, you hear a noise. *"Awroo!"*

"They have dogs after us!" says John. "Let's go."

You're curious about this Maroon town and about Nanny, but you could jump back in time. How about Port Royal in 1670, when it was a buccaneer capital? It's hard to tell how either choice would get you closer to finding the treasure, so you'll just have to make a guess!

Follow John to Maroon Town. Turn to page 82.

Jump back to buccaneer time. Turn to page 100.

You feel the tip of the pirate captain's sword pressing against your throat.

"Well?" he says. "Your minute is almost up!" Your sailors stand there watching you.

You've lost your ship, so you might as well make the best of it. Easy come, easy go! You reach up and push the blade away.

"Fine," you say. "It's a pirate's life for me!"

Captain Bannister smiles. He turns to face his crew and stabs his sword into the wooden deck.

"This ship is ours!" he shouts. "All who wish to join our band may do so. We sail today for Hispaniola, to repair our ships at Samana Bay!"

Samana Bay? That's where your friend Phips stays when he searches for the *Concepcion*. You hope the pirates don't get him!

Luckily the bay is empty when you arrive. Captain Bannister sails right onto the beach. With long ropes you help pull the two ships over onto their sides. You scrape the barnacles off their hulls, so they can glide faster through the sea.

Turn to page 80.

You're standing in the sandy streets of Port Royal, Jamaica, February 1692. The town is still full of noisy sailors bars.

You feel a strange rumbling beneath your feet. The ground is vibrating! Houses around you crack and rattle. You hear an odd, low whooshing sound.

"Earthquake!" someone screams. The ground seems to pull itself right out from under your feet. The edge of the town slips and disappears into the sea. You were standing in the middle of a town, but now you're lying by the edge of the ocean!

The vibrations die down. The water slips away, as if the tide is going out in fast motion. Ruined docks and houses appear again as the water disappears.

People are screaming. Others are numb with shock. "Look!" someone cries. "Out to sea!" There's a wave speeding toward you. Not just a wave: a solid wall of water fifty feet high. It's a tidal wave, about to bury Port Royal forever!

Jump back to safety in New Providence, 1684. Turn to page 50.

f you're certain ye want to join us," a pirate says, "come this way." He takes you to where Captain Joseph Bannister sits by a table on the beach. Bannister throws a piece of parchment on the table.. "If you want to be a pirate," he says, "you must sign this, like everyone else."

"What does it say?"

"If we find no prey, you get no pay. But if we do, every sailor gets a share. You, because you're young, get half a share. But you'll have to earn it! Do you agree so far?"

You nod.

"If one of your arms or legs gets shot off, you get two hundred pieces of eight extra. For a finger or an eye, one hundred." He points to his black eye patch so you'll understand. "We want no cowards on our ship! If you run away from battle or if you steal, you'll be marooned on a lonely island."

He hands you a quill pen made out of a long feather.

"If you can't write, you can just mark an *X*."

You dip the quill in ink and write "Lucky Century" on the dotted line.

Your search for the *Concepcion* can wait. You're a pirate!

Turn to page 91.

All night you run through the woods of Jamaica. The hunting dogs follow. *"Awroo! Awroo!"*

John grabs you by the shoulder. "Stop!" He examines the trail ahead of you. He bypasses the trail for a few yards, then gets back on again. You follow.

"Watch!" He points back down the trail.

"Awroo!" The dogs come running after you, with a hunter close behind. Then the ground seems to disappear beneath their feet. They fall into a pit! The pit is lined with sharp wooden spikes pointed up. Dogs and hunters scream as they fall right on the spikes.

You look at John. "If you hadn't grabbed me when you did—" You gulp. "Thanks!"

John smiles and holds up his left arm. "This hand that grabbed you? This hand is yours. Forever!"

"Who set that trap?" you wonder.

"The Maroons did," John explains. "We must be getting close to their town."

The path goes up along a steep cliff. *THWAP!* A spear sticks quivering in the path

ahead of you. Another one sticks behind you. You're surrounded!

"Who are you?" asks a man carrying a rifle. "What do you want?" He wears a leather loin-cloth. His hair is tied in closely knotted rows.

"I'm a runaway slave," says John. "We want to join the Maroons."

"Who's that with you?"

"A runaway servant. My friend, who saved my life."

"Huh. Come. Nanny will test you. If you are lying, you will die!" They take you up the narrow path. At the top of the cliff you see a clearing, with grass-roofed huts built in a circle. Runaway slaves have built a village just like the ones they left back in Africa!

The men push you inside one of the huts. A woman with a colored scarf around her head sits with her back to you. She throws some powder in a little fire, and the dark hut fills with a strange smell.

"They call me Nanny," she says slowly.

"We are . . ." John starts to say.

"Silence! I know who you are." She waves her hand. "John. You wish to join the free Maroons. Will you swear to fight bravely, obey our laws, and never tell anyone our secrets?"

"Yes," John says.

"Good. Go. Tell the ones outside that you will take the test of strength and will." John gets up and leaves. You sit there for a long time, watching her back.

"You," she says quietly. "You I must touch with my eyes." She turns around. Her face is painted gray, like ashes.

"Come closer." She sprinkles powder on your shoulder, then reaches up and pulls out a lock of your hair!

"Ow!"

"So. You can be hurt, like all the sun's children. But still you are a great sorcerer." She lights the hair on fire, and breathes the smoke in deeply.

"You are a great traveler. Sometimes you travel like other men. But sometimes"—she stares into your eyes—"sometimes, the sun comes up. She looks for all her children, but you are gone! What are you searching for? Don't tell me."

She closes her eyes, and rocks back and forth. "I see a ship," she says in a strange, high voice. "A great ship, like the one that brought me from Africa. It is very heavy. In its belly are many stones the color of a white man in his grave. Silver! A storm. The ship hits a reef."

"That's what I'm looking for!" you say. "But where is the reef the *Concepcion* hit?"

She smiles. "Let me tell you a story. Anansi, the giant spider, one day she went walking on the sea. Every step that spider took, she left an island for a footprint! White men call those islands many things. Bahama, Turks, Caicos. Handkercher. Then that spider settle down to sleep. Where she sleep they now call Hispaniola." She opens her eyes. "But how many steps that spider take before she sleep? How many islands swimming in that sea?"

You'll have to check your map. What is the meaning of her riddle? If there is another reef to the east of Handkercher, maybe *that's* where the *Concepcion* is. Maybe you should jump ahead a few months and meet Captain Phips in Port Royal. But what will you tell him?

"You, sorcerer traveler," says Nanny. "You may dance with us Maroons, raid plantation with us. Or you may go, in your special way."

"But which way is best?" you ask.

She takes something red and smears it on one of your hands. In the other hand she puts a pinch of salt. "Short road," she says, "bring blood. Long road bring sweat. Which will it be, sorcerer?"

Dance and raid with the Maroons. Turn to page 110.

Jump ahead to meet Phips. Turn to page 96.

he huge, blood-covered man comes toward you. His long knife shines in the sun.

"Thank you very much," you say slowly. You back away. "That pig almost got me!"

"You thank me?" he says in a deep voice. He comes closer.

"It is I who should thank you!" He reaches down with his knife and cuts the pig's skin from nose to tail. "These boar-pig, he are hard to catch. You bring him out in sun for Pierre to shoot. Good work!" He pulls the pig's guts out and starts slicing up the meat.

"You want to be my partner?" He holds out a hand dripping with blood. You think for a moment, then shake it. "Bring me some leaves. Big ones. Green." You help him wrap the meat in leaves.

"Do you want some new shoes?"

What? New shoes! You shake your head no.

"Good. I need some myself." He strips the skin off the pig's leg and sticks his foot into the skin. He ties up the hole below his toe and proudly shows you his new shoe, dripping with blood.

"This way!" You follow him through the woods, carrying a load of sliced pig. The jungle you were so lost in seems like home to him. Soon you come to a sort of camp. Other men dressed just as strangely as Pierre throw green wood on big, smoky fires. Strips of meat hang above the fire on big wooden racks.

"On these racks we smoke our meat," says Pierre, "to keep it fresh. Then we can sell to ships." He gives you a piece. It's tough and smoky.

"The Indians taught us how. The rack is called a boucan, and we are boucaniers."

That must be where the word "buccaneer" comes from.

"Some of us were shipwrecked here. Others were slaves or servants, and run away. It is hard life, but soon it changes. Come!"

He takes you down a winding path to the sea. A small boat sits on the edge of the beach.

"My friends and I, we are sick of chasing pigs. The Spanish hunt us, just as we hunt pigs. And all the time they sail past, in their ships almost sinking with treasure. Tonight, *we* sail, to seek our fortune!"

"Where will you go?"

"Northeast. This island is Hispaniola. When ships pass, they must stay close, because of dangerous reefs to the north. And who will be waiting for them, right in the middle?"

"You."

He laughs and gives you a bear hug. Boy, does he smell!

"Right, my partner. Big Pierre, he knows these reefs like the back of a pig!"

You look at the tiny boat and imagine drifting on the wide, wide sea. You don't have to go—you could go off in the woods and jump to another place and time. How about Jamaica?

 Jump ahead 30 years to the pirate city of Port Royal, Jamaica. Turn to page 100.

 Sail with Pierre. Turn to page 103.

The pirate captain's sword still presses against your throat.

"I don't want to be a pirate," you say.

Joseph Bannister's eyes show surprise. "You are very brave," he says, "but also very foolish."

His men run a rope all the way under the ship and tie your arms to one end of it. Men on the other side of the ship lean over the side and give a tug, laughing when the rope nearly pulls you overboard. Bannister pushes you out on a plank stuck over the side, prodding with his sword.

"Walk the plank, my young foolish friend. Jump, before the rope pulls you off!"

"Heave!" the pirates shout as they yank the other end of the rope. It pulls you off! You land with a splash in the sea. The rope is pulling you under! You scrape along the sharp, stony barnacles growing on the ship's bottom. It's dark and gloomy down here, and you're running out of air.

Well, you aren't getting any closer to the treasure this way. Jump in time, before you're keelhauled for good!

Jump back a year to safety in Vera Cruz. Turn to page 20.

You step out on the deck of the *Golden Fleece* as the sun rises over the horizon. You almost walk on the body of a pirate. Men lie sprawling everywhere. What happened? Could you have slept right through a battle the night before?

Captain Bannister comes out, rubbing his eyes. "Look at this!" he says with disgust. He kicks one of the men, who swears and gets groggily to his feet.

"Wake up, you drunkards!" shouts Bannister. "The Spanish rum we captured is too good for you. Raise the sails! There'll be plenty of good drink when we reach Tortuga!"

The men complain and rub their heads.

"Let's have a song," someone suggests as you pull the long ropes to raise the heavy sails.

"Yo *ho*, and up she rises! Yo *ho*, and up she rises, yo *ho*, and up she rises early in the morning!" With each line of the song you give a pull, and a sail inches its way up the mast.

One pirate refuses to wake up.

"What shall we do with a drunken sailor," they chant, "early in the morning?"

"Why don't we pour water on him?" you suggest. They laugh. Someone gets a barrel as the rest of you pull.

"Pull out the plug and wet him all over, pull out the plug and wet him all over early in the morning!" The soaking pirate jumps up, sputtering, and the rest of them laugh. By the end of the song, the wind is pushing the ship along. You glide along the north coast of Hispaniola.

"Look there!" someone yells. "More prey!" A small ship enters the mouth of Samana Bay. The two pirate ships turn to chase it.

Does that ship belong to Captain Phips? You hope not. His ships are equipped for treasure hunting, not fighting.

The pirate ships sail around a bend, looking for the little ship.

Uh-oh! The little ship has big friends! Hiding there waiting for you are two fully armed warships.

"It's a trap!" cries Bannister. "The king's warships sent to destroy us."

"Let's run for it, Captain," says a gunner. "We've already got plenty of plunder."

"Run? Never!" says the pirate captain. He runs to the side of the ship. "Who dares lie in wait for the dreaded *Golden Fleece*?" he shouts.

The captain of the closest warship shouts back. "I am Captain Spragge of the frigate *Drake*. Loyal servant of Charles, king of England. Surrender, or I'll blast you out of the water!"

"You!" Bannister laughs. "You are a sneaking puppy! Like anyone who lets rich men buy their service. The rich men rob the poor under the cover of law, while *we* plunder the rich under the protection of our own courage! Why don't *you* join *us*?"

"My conscience," says Spragge, "will not let me break the laws of God and man."

"Well, then," Bannister replies, waving his sword, "you have a devil for a conscience. And I am a *free* prince of the sea! I have as much authority to make war on the whole world as those who have a hundred ships at sea!" He turns to his crew. "Gunners, fire at will!"

The gunners light the cannons' fuses, and a volley of cannonballs flies off. Shots fly back the other way. They crash through the side of your ship, rip through sails, and snap masts in two.

You're put to work loading up a cannon with cannonballs. Something hot and flaming whizzes past your ear. They're shooting flaming arrows at the ship! The foresail is already aflame.

"She's going under," someone yells. "Abandon ship!"

You hurry to the longboat and push off. One of the warships cuts you off.

"Will you surrender now?" shouts Captain Spragge. "In the name of King Charles, surrender, or we'll blow you to smithereens!"

You put up your hands. Soldiers come down to haul you aboard. They lock you in chains in the hold of the *Drake* with other groaning pirates. You hear the boom of cannons and the sound of guns, but no one will tell you what's going on.

After a day in chains in the dark, Spragge's men drag you up on deck. The sunlight hurts your eyes after your sitting so long in darkness.

There's something swinging from the long poles that hold up the sails. The bodies of Joseph Bannister and his officers dangle by the neck in the wind.

The soldiers take off your chains and give you a mop. "Clean the blood off this deck," they command.

As you wipe the deck, you find yourself behind a pile of sails where no one can see you. Time to get back on the trail of silver! Jump in time to meet up with the *Concepcion*.

 Jump back forty-three years to Havana, Cuba. Turn to page 14.

t's June 12, 1684. You're wandering through Port Royal, Jamaica, looking for Captain Phips. There he is! You run up to him.

"Captain!" you call. "Sir! I know where the ship went down. We can find the treasure now."

"Oh, do you now? That's interesting. Where?"

"It's further east from where you were looking. It's northeast of Isabela, Hispaniola."

Phips scratches his head. "Further east, eh? Well, I don't know how we'll find it, then. It's supposed to be on a reef."

"That's just it. It must be—"

"Wait a moment, my young friend. Just where did you get this valuable information? You've only been on shore leave for two hours!"

You stare at him. Two hours! Of course. As far as he knows, you just got off the *Rose of Algeree* a little while ago. And you can't tell him about all the searching you've been doing!

"Well, uh," you say, "I ran into a sailor in a bar. He has a friend who was a survivor of the wreck. . . ."

"Ho! I've heard that one before." He looks at the friend he's walking with. They smile. "Every sailor in Port Royal claims he knows a survivor of that wreck." He puts his arm around your shoulders. "Don't go believing the tall tales of old sailors. Now run along. I'm hiring a new crew, and we sail soon for Samana Bay!"

"But—"

"That's enough. Run along!"

That makes you angry. Somehow you'll have to find proof that you know what you're talking about. But how? You're stalking along, thinking, when you bump into somebody.

You look up. It's that nasty kid Teal! He stares at you in amazement. Better run for it!

He chases you, shouting. "Stop, thief! Police!"

A pair of arms grabs you and lifts you off the ground.

"Aha!" cries the policeman who locked you up the last time. "There you are. How did you get out of our jail?" He drags you off to the same gloomy prison.

"The penalty for running away from your master," the policeman says, "we leave up to him. But first, we're going to find out who helped you escape. Tie the rascal to the rack, boys!" They tie your feet to the bottom of a big square torture machine. Your arms they tie, too, high above your head. The ropes are wound around a big wheel.

"Turn the crank," the policeman snarls. As the crank turns, the ropes around your arms and legs begin to pull you apart!

"Well? How did you escape?"

Ow! They're pulling your arms right out of their sockets!

"What's the matter, rogue? Trying to *stretch* the truth? Ha ha ha! Now we'll let you *rack* your brains for a few minutes before we turn the crank some more!" They go out of the room, laughing at their own cruel jokes.

Time to get out of here! You think back over the places you've been, the times you've explored. You could try someplace new—or you could go back to a place you've already been to see if there's anything you missed.

Ride the *Concepcion* from Havana, 1641. Turn to page 14.

Explore the jungles of Hispaniola, 1641. Turn to page 70.

Comb the beaches of New Providence, 1684. Turn to page 50.

Visit one of the Virgin Islands, 1684. Turn to page 66.

ou're in Port Royal, Jamaica. It's August 12, 1670. Sailors roam the streets, drinking and singing songs with their arms around the waists of women in brightly colored gowns.

"A toast!" shouts a sailor. "To Captain Henry Morgan, leader of the raid on Venezuela that has filled our pockets with gold!"

"Yer pockets," says a redheaded woman, "ain't filled anymore, are they? Ye've spent it all already."

"They'll be filled again soon enough, my sweet. We sail again in two days, for Vaca Island. I bet old Henry Morgan has a trick or two up his sleeve!"

The buccaneers are going to meet at Vaca Island. If that's near Hispaniola, you could sail with them and search for the treasure there.

A pirate with a keg blocks your path. "Drink," he commands. "Everyone must be as drunk as I am."

"No thanks," you say politely. He pulls out a gun and points it at you!

"So! Ye refuse a friendly invitation? How insulting!"

"I didn't mean to insult you!" you say quickly.

"Then drink!" he roars, holding out a mug. "Now!"

You take a sip. Ugh. It smells like moldy potatoes. You pretend to drink it down, while he roars and splashes everyone around with wine.

"Finished?" he says. "Good. Prove it! Turn the mug upside down over your head."

What do you do now? He scowls, and fires his gun right over your head! You turn the mug over, drenching yourself with sticky wine.

"Faker!" the pirate roars. He pours another.

Time to get out of here! Should you jump ahead a couple of days and sail with Henry Morgan? Or should you jump to 1692? By then, somebody here ought to know where the treasure is—Phips will already have found it.

You take off down the street and turn a corner. Good! No one around. "Drink!" you hear the pirate bellow far behind you. "Or the streets will drink your blood!"

 Jump to Port Royal, 1692. Turn to page 78.

 Jump two days ahead to sail with Morgan. Turn to page 106.

ou've been waiting in Pierre's boat for a week now for a ship to pass through the channel north of Hispaniola. You ate the last strip of boucan meat two days before, but Big Pierre refuses to give up.

"Pierre!" says one of the buccaneers, "we have no food! How can we fight if we are weak from starvation?"

Pierre growls. "You can't wait to eat the fine food of the Spanish, dog?" He takes off a pig-skin shoe and throws it to the man. "There, chew on that!"

"Here comes a ship!" someone says. "At last." On the horizon you see a sail. The men cheer, and they sharpen their knives. Then another ship appears, and another. It's a whole fleet!

"This is not so good," says Pierre. "They have many guns. A small boat with only twenty-eight men has no chance against a fleet! We will pretend to be fishermen." The ships sail on, and soon you can see the people on them. Pierre holds a long pole from the boat's stern, as if he's fishing.

"They look at us with spyglasses. Everyone smile. Wave! Wave to the pretty ships!" The dirty, bearded buccaneers all grin with their yellow teeth and wave. One ship turns to come closer.

BOOM! Something splashes in the water a few yards away. Pierre drops his pole.

"They fire on us! The dogs! Quick, we will hide in the reefs. We are small, the rocks are no problem. The Spanish cannot follow."

You turn the boat and row with all your strength. Cannonballs splash all around you. Soon the boat is gliding between jagged chunks of coral. It all looks familiar.

"Is this the Handkercher Reef?" you ask.

"No. The Handkercher Reef is farther to the west. This is another reef, northwest from Samana Bay." Hmmm, you think. Very interesting. Maybe the ship went down in *this* reef, and Captain Phips doesn't know about it.

The fleet sails off to the east, and Pierre brings his boat back into the channel. The sun is going down. You sail southwest, toward the old Spanish ghost town of Isabela on Hispaniola.

"Well," says Pierre, "our luck is not so good this time. Next year. . ."

"Don't give up yet, Big Pierre. Look!" One more ship is coming up the channel. All its sails are out as it struggles to catch up with the fleet.

"Aha!" says Pierre. "Perfect. My partner,"

he says to you, "take this tool. Drill a hole in
the bottom of your boat."

"A hole?" you ask.

"Yes. There will be no escape for us! Either
we take this Spanish ship or we die. Now,
quiet."

You do as he tells you. Water trickles in and
floods the bottom of the boat. It's dark now.
You see lights on the ship above the huge,
black hull. You can hear someone laughing on
deck. Your boat, rapidly sinking, is so small!
How will you ever capture such a big ship?
Maybe you should slip over the side of the boat
in the darkness and jump in time—perhaps to
Samana Bay, not far away, to wait for Captain
Phips.

"My buccaneers!" whispers Big Pierre.
"Soon it will be our turn to laugh. But we must
be brave. I want you to swear, all of you, a
solemn oath. We will fight to the last man.
Will you swear?"

"Aye," whispers each man in turn. You,
however, are not so sure you want to join this
desperate party.

Stay with Pierre. Turn to page 107.

Jump ahead forty-three years to look for Phips in Semana Bay. Turn to page 112.

ugust 14, 1670. You're watching ships load up with sailors in Port Royal, Jamaica.

"We're off to raid the Spanish, mates!" Captain Henry Morgan shouts to the crowd. "Buccaneers from all over the Caribbee are meeting us at Vaca Island. This will be the biggest raid of my career."

"My dear friend Henry!" interrupts a man in a feathered hat.

"Well, now, this is an honor," says Morgan. "What brings our distinguished governor to see us?"

"News from London," says the governor of Jamaica. "We've just signed a treaty in Madrid. England and Spain are no longer at war!"

Morgan stares. "Peace?" He looks around at his disappointed buccaneers. "Well, isn't it too bad the news arrived just *after* we left Port Royal?"

"But, Henry . . ."

"Never ye worry, Tommy me lad! We'll keep your share of the plunder safe. All aboard!"

You sail with Morgan. He's going near Hispaniola. Somehow you may find a clue to the treasure there.

Turn to page 121.

You're standing in the darkness on a sinking boat. Above you, Pierre climbs up the side of the Spanish ship. He tosses down a ladder made of rope. You climb up into the blackness.

"Hurry!" hisses Pierre. "Soon will come the next guard." One by one the buccaneers slip over the side, carrying their knives between their teeth.

"Half of you capture the gun room. Partner, come with me." You creep across the deck. A guard sits on a barrel outside the captain's cabin. You hear singing and the clink of glasses from inside.

"Count to fifteen," whispers Pierre, "and then whistle. Like a bird." He disappears.

You count and then whistle. The guard stands up and peers in your direction. There's Pierre! He slips a cord around the guard's neck and pulls. The guard struggles and slumps to the deck.

"Now!" says Pierre. He throws open the door and you rush in. The officers sit there in their underwear, playing cards.

"Aiee! Jesus bless us! Are these devils, or what are they?"

"We are the spirit of revenge!" cries Pierre. He holds a pistol to the captain's chest. "Surrender your ship or your life!"

You hear gunfire and the sound of crossing swords. One of the officers jumps for the door, but a buccaneer runs him through with his blade. Another man runs in, missing an ear.

"Three men lost, Big Pierre, but the ship's guns are ours!"

"What say you, Spanish captain? Are you captain still?"

"I—I—the ship is yours!"

You lock the Spanish soldiers up, and the buccaneers man the sails.

The ship contains little silver but many kinds of expensive colored dyes. Pierre decides to sail to his native France to sell them, but you decide to get back on the trail of your own treasure.

On his way to France, Pierre stops at one of the small Virgin Islands. He keeps only as many sailors as he needs and leaves the rest of the Spanish on the island. You take the opportunity to wander off to the woods and jump ahead in time.

Jump to the future of this island. Turn to page 66.

You're awakened by the sound of beating drums. You've slept all day in the Maroon village, and it's night again. Outside, the runaway slaves are dancing in a circle.

"Shout, obeah, shout!" they sing. "Shout, I tell you shout. Obeah!" Your friend John steps out of the circle when he sees you.

"Century! Come and dance! We're getting ready for a raid!" He pulls you up to the circle.

"Rock, obeah, rock! Rock, I tell you, rock." The music sounds strangely familiar. Here you are in Jamaica in 1684, dancing to African music, and it sounds like rock and roll!

"Gimme the kneebone bend, obeah! Gimme the kneebone bend." You dance with your knees bent almost to the ground. You feel strange. This dancing is going to your head!

A woman with a necklace of human teeth falls into the center of the circle. She shrieks, twitching and hopping as if she's crazy. Then she starts talking, very calmly, with the voice of an old man! The older dancers seem to be listening to what she says, but you can't understand.

"What's she saying?" you ask John.

"I don't know. She's speaking an African language. But she doesn't know that language. The spirit of somebody dead is talking through her mouth!"

This is getting weird.

A dancer steps out in the middle with a gun. He pretends to shoot the other dancers. They pretend to catch the bullets and throw them back at him. He falls, "killed" by his own bullets. The dance ends as the Maroons who are going raiding wave their rifles in the air.

 Go on a Maroon raid. Turn to page 115.

ou're alone by the edge of Samana Bay, Hispaniola. It's February 4, 1684. Captain Phips hasn't shown up yet. You could jump a few months ahead, but you shouldn't go looking for him until you're sure you know what to tell him.

"Oooo. Eeeeee!" A high voice comes from the wood. "Is it a ghost," it wails, "that I seeee?"

"Who's there?" you cry.

"Don Villavicencioooo," the cracked voice sings, "has gone beloooow. Who's left? First one, now twoooo!"

Villavicencio! He was the admiral aboard the *Concepcion*. Maybe this is a survivor of the wreck! You pluck up your courage and go into the forest. You see a strange old man who disappears into a cave.

"Who are you?" you call into the mouth of the cave. The old hermit comes out slowly.

"Don't you remember meee? I remember youuu!" he sings. "East, south, west. Who remembers best?"

You look closely at his face. It's the pilot of the *Concepcion*! Has he been hiding here for forty years?

"I have a question," you say. "Did the *Concepcion* sink in the Handkercher Reef?"

114

"The Handkercher!" he laughs. He slaps his knee, chooses a direction, and spits.

"The east wind spits in your handkercher. The east wind spits a ship!" he cries. "But it's not in the Handkercher, nooo. It's in the spit. The ship is in the spit!" He dances with glee and runs back in his cave.

Well. More riddles! Pierre told you there were reefs further east than the ones Phips knows about. Could the pilot be saying that the ship went down in these unknown and unnamed reefs? Maybe.

You look at the sea. Two ships sail into the bay. Is it Phips? You run down to meet them. The ships sail right onto a beach, and the sailors pull them over on their sides with long ropes.

"Scratch him on his belly with a rusty razor," they sing as they pull. "Early in the morning. Yo ho!"

It's not Phips. It's a pair of pirate ships. You talk with some of the pirates, who seem like a fun-loving crew. Should you join them, or jump ahead a few months to meet Captain Phips?

 Sail with pirates. Turn to page 80.

 Jump ahead to look for Phips. Turn to page 116.

You're creeping through the woods, sneaking up on a plantation. You reach a shed and peer around it. The buildings look familiar. It's Throneberry's place, the one you just escaped from!

"John!" you hiss. "Why did we come back *here*?"

"I led us here. We're going to free my sisters."

The maroon leader hands you a burning torch. "You, Century. Stay here. Set fire this shed. People come to put him fire out, we be raidin' slave house." They disappear into the night.

Someone's coming. You jump inside the shed and close the door. A familiar smell surrounds you. You're in an outhouse!

"Hurry up in there," a voice says. It's the slavedriver! You hold the torch to the roof. The little room fills up with smoke.

"What's going on in there?"

There! It's finally burning. The slavedriver starts kicking the door in. You've got to get out of here!

 Jump back in time to Port Royal, 1670. Turn to page 100.

t's June 23, 1684. You see two ships at anchor out in Samana Bay. There's Phips loading water kegs on the beach!

"Blow me down," he says, "if it isn't young Lucky Century. What are *you* doing here?"

"I've been doing research for you, Captain. Now I'm *sure* I know where the treasure lies!"

He crosses his arms and looks skeptical. "You do, eh? Well, let's hear your tale."

"I met a buccaneer," you say, "who sails around here a lot. He told me there's another reef to the east of Handkercher Reef."

Phips looks surprised. "Another reef? It's not on my charts!"

"That's not all. Back in the woods here there's a crazy old hermit. He was the pilot of the *Concepcion*! He went into hiding to keep from being hanged for losing the ship. He says the same thing: the ship is east of Handkercher."

The captain grabs your shoulders with both hands. "Now, this is interesting. If it's true, my young friend, you shall have a double share in the treasure!"

You board Phips's ship and sail down the bay.

Soon the ships are anchored safely off the reef. Canoes paddle off in all directions, weaving in and out between the rocks and towers of coral. You paddle in the front of your canoe with first mate Francis Rogers. You stop from time to time to examine the sea floor below.

"Well, no luck," says Rogers. "It's getting late. Let's go back."

"Wait," you say. Up ahead you see three rocks that look very familiar. "Let's try up there." You paddle closer.

"Do you see any treasure?" Rogers asks.

"No," you say, "no treasure. But I wonder who's been throwing cannons in the water?"

"Cannons?" he cries. "The ship's guns. We found it!"

Rogers stays in the boat while you dive. The cannons lie on white sand. The ship has long since rotted away, but you can see the outline of the bow on the sea floor. You can't see any silver, just a lot of black, coral-covered rocks. You have just enough time to grab a couple of these and kick madly up to the air.

"Hmm," Rogers says. "Funny sort of rock." He hits them together. They break apart— into chunks of silver coins.

"Yahoo!" you cry, and dive back into the sea.

It's easier to get the silver now that the ship has rotted away, but diving thirty feet is tiring. You put the silver in a sack and paddle back to the ship. The other searchers are all reporting back. Rogers puts his finger to his lips.

"Nothing to southwards, Cap'n," says one.

"No luck in our canoe, neither."

"It's got to be here somewhere," mutters Phips. He pounds his fist on the table. "We're going to find it if it takes all summer! How about you, Century?"

"We didn't find much," you say casually. "Just this." You pull a silver bar out of the sack. Everyone stands staring at it. No one can speak. Then Phips gets down on his knees. You all kneel with him.

"Merciful God," he says quietly, "we thank thee for blessing thy humble servants with success." Then he jumps to his feet.

"Yahoo!" Everyone shouts and dances around the room. Phips brings out a keg of brandy, and everyone toasts your health. The captain gives you a hug, tears of joy streaming down his face.

In the next few days, you load hundreds of pounds of silver on the ship. Only the professional divers have the strength to go down that deep, over and over again. They bring up bucketfuls of silver coins, tons of silver bars, spoons, forks, candlesticks, and bowls.

"My dear friend Century," Phips says, "we owe you so much! You'll be rich when we get back to London. But I'll make you a present now. You may have as much silver as will fit in your knapsack."

You choose some nice thick candlesticks as a present for your family. For yourself you choose all sorts of coins with the names of different kings on them.

You've fulfilled your mission. It's time for the traveler to return.

 Jump 400 years to the twentieth century. Turn to page 123.

It's night time. You're standing guard outside a cabin on Henry Morgan's ship. Buccaneer captains from a dozen different ships are meeting here, off a small island near Hispaniola, to decide which Spanish towns to raid. They've been shouting at each other for over an hour.

The door bursts open. Henry Morgan runs out, chasing a French buccaneer with a sword.

"I'm master here!" Morgan roars. "And I say we go to Panama."

"But Maracaibo is so much easier!"

"Idiot! I just raided Maracaibo last year. They'll still be licking their wounds." He calls to his friends. "Lock these Frenchies up!" Guards drag the French captains off. You stay with Morgan, who stamps around the room smashing things with his sword.

"I'm sick to death of this parlay-voo," he storms. "We'll take the Frenchy ships with us!"

KABOOM! An enormous explosion rocks the ship. You're thrown into the blackness and land with a splash in the sea. The ship has split in two. The angry Frenchmen must have set fire to the gunpowder room!

"Help!" a sailor calls, splashing about. "I can't swim!" It seems crazy to be a sailor and not know how to swim, but sailors are drowning all around you. You paddle over to the nearest one.

"Let me help you," you say. He grabs you! You try to push him off, but he hangs on like a madman. He's so desperate for safety that he's going to drown you, too.

The only way out is to jump in time. You're close to Hispaniola—so the *Concepcion* went down somewhere nearby.

Jump back 30 years to the island of Hispaniola. Turn to page 70.

What's this? You're not home yet! You're still looking out at the treasure reef, but it's November 30, 1978. You're on a modern ship! There's a radar scope on top, and all sorts of sophisticated diving gear on the deck. Divers in rubber suits bob about in the water.

"Hello! I haven't seen you before." A smiling man in a modern sailor's cap shakes your hand. "Are you with the newspaper reporters?"

"Actually," you say, "I'm sort of a—researcher."

"Ha! That means you're a treasure hunter, like us. Well, you're just in time! Burt Webber, the leader of our expedition, thinks we've found the wreck of the *Concepcion*—the same wreck old Captain Phips found four hundred years ago."

"I've heard of Phips," you say. "Whatever happened to him?"

"Of course you've heard of Phips! He's the inspiration for all us treasure hunters. Well, he became a rich man, of course, and so famous the king of England made him governor of Massachusetts."

He waves at the divers. "I've often wondered how he found that wreck. We've been searching for it for years, and we have all sorts of fancy equipment he didn't have."

"If Phips found the silver," you ask, "aren't you afraid there's nothing left?"

"That's possible, yes. But there was a lot of silver on that ship. I'm guessing Phips just didn't get it all." Somebody signals to him. He puts on a diving suit and jumps in the water.

For his sake, you hope he's right. You can still see the same three rocks on the reef.

Uh-oh. Phips found his treasure on the other side of those rocks. Should you tell the divers? Then you remember—Phips found the *bow* of the ship. Maybe the *stern* is over here! If so, Webber's crew may find more treasure than Phips did.

A diver comes to the surface, waving something in his hand.

"A Spanish coin," he cries, "dated 1639. We've found it!" Everyone cheers.

You watch them load silver onto the ship. They have a lot less trouble than Phips did. They have pumps that suck up the bottom and spit out silver on the ship.

A crew of sailors from the navy of the Dominican Republic count every piece of silver the divers find. Half the treasure belongs to them, because the reef is in their waters.

You're looking through the mess when you notice one of the sailors eyeing your heavy knapsack. If he sees your silver, he'll think

you've stolen it! You wander off, whistling, and find an empty room.

Time to jump—home! You think about your adventures in the 1600s: the swordfights, the scurvy, the slavery, the sad lives you've seen and the happy ones. An exciting time to live in, but dangerous. As you jump for the last time, you wonder if you were, indeed, born in a Lucky Century.

MISSION COMPLETED.

DATA FILE

About the Contributors

JIM GASPERINI reviewed interactive computer fiction for *Electronic Fun*, and published the history of a medieval French artisan's guild in *Museum*. He has been a videotape editor, a busker, a traveling book salesman, and a literary agent, and made his operatic debut in the 1983 Metropolitan Opera production of Don Carlo as Arquebusier (spear carrier). He resides in New York. He is the author of Time Machine 1, *Secret of the Knights*.

ALEX NINO is an internationally respected illustrator. His work has appeared in such publications as *Metal Hurlant* in France and *Starlog* in America, and in hundreds of magazines in his native Philippines. His paintings and illustrations have been published as portfolios, book jackets, and graphic stories. He is also the winner of an Inkpot Award.

JOHN PIERARD is a free-lance illustrator living in Manhattan. He is best known for his science fiction and fantasy illustrations for *Isaac Asimov's Science Fiction Magazine, Distant Stars,* and SPI games such as Universe. He was a contributing artist to *The Secret*, a Bantam Book. He is allegedly descended from pirates.